First published in the UK in 2005 by
QED Publishing
A Quarto Group company
226 City Road
London EC1V 2TT
www.qed-publishing.co.uk

A Catalogue record for this book is available from the British Library.

ISBN 1 84538 456 3

Written by Wendy Body
Designed by Alix Wood
Editor Hannah Ray
Illustrated by Sanja Rescek

Series Consultant Anne Faundez
Publisher Steve Evans
Creative Director Louise Morley
Editorial Manager Jean Coppendale

Printed and bound in China

QED
Word Banks

MINKI'S
Day

Wendy Body

QED Publishing

QED

At **seven o'clock**, I got up and I dressed,
I decided I wanted to look my best.

seven o'clock

5

At **eight o'clock**, still tidy and neat,
breakfast was ready so I sat down to eat.

eight o'clock

At **nine o'clock**, I was in a bad mood,
my lovely clean t-shirt was spattered with food.

nine o'clock

9

At **ten o'clock**, my pet was a-quiver,
so I took him out for a walk by the river.
But I got all muddy and started to shiver
when he pulled me over and I fell in the river.

ten o'clock

11

At **twelve o'clock**, I was safely back home,
for lunch I had soup and my pet had a bone.

twelve o'clock

At **two o'clock**, it was time to help Dad.
He tried very hard but his painting
was bad.

two o'clock

15

At **five o'clock**, it was time for our tea ... Mum tripped over my pet and spilled custard on me.

five o'clock

17

By **six o'clock**, I'd had quite enough
of falling in rivers and that sort of stuff.
I'd even had custard spilled over my head,
so I jumped in the bath and then went to bed!

six o'clock

Things to do

Can you point to the times to go with the clocks?

At      Minki got dressed.

At      Minki had breakfast.

At      Minki went for a walk.

At      Minki had lunch.

At      Minki helped Dad.

At      Minki had tea.

five o'clock	two o'clock
seven o'clock	eight o'clock
ten o'clock	twelve o'clock

Things to do

Can you work out how these food words begin?

Can you think of some more food words?
How do they begin?

Word bank

Words from the story

bath

bed

bone

breakfast

custard

Dad

dressed

eat

food

lunch

Mum

o'clock

painting

pet

river

soup

tea

t-shirt

22

Word bank

Words to do with time

early   late
morning   afternoon
evening   night
yesterday   tomorrow
            today
day   week
month   year

More words to do with time

quarter past
quarter to
half past

quarter past seven

quarter to four

half past ten

Parents' and teachers' notes

- As you read the book to your child, run your finger along underneath the text. This will help your child to follow the reading and focus on the look of the words as well as their sound.

- The story in this book is told as much through the illustrations as the text so it is essential to help your child to understand the pictures. Use open-ended questions to encourage your child to respond, e.g. 'What's happening on this page?'

- Once your child is familiar with the book, encourage him or her to join in with the reading – especially the times of the day.

- Can your child remember what Minki did at particular times of the day?

- Encourage your child to express opinions and preferences, e.g. ask questions such as, 'Which picture do you think is the funniest? Why?' 'Which part of the day do you think Minki disliked most? Why?'

- Ask your child to make comparisons between Minki and themselves, e.g. 'At eight o'clock Minki had breakfast. What time did you have your breakfast today?' Discuss what your child might do over the course of a day. Are there certain things he or she does at particular times?

- Talk about Minki's pet and think of a name for it. Encourage your child to invent and describe a monster pet of his or her own.

- Draw your child's attention to the meaning and spelling of some words, e.g. 'breakfast', 'lunch', 'quiver', 'shiver'.

- Look at the 'Things to do' pages (pages 20–21). Read the questions to your child and help where necessary. Give lots of encouragement. Even if your child gets something wrong you can say, 'That was a great try but it's not that one it's this one'.

- Read and discuss the words on the 'Word bank' pages (pages 22–23). Look at the letter patterns and how the words are spelled. Cover up the first part of a word and see if your child can remember what was there. Can your child write the simpler words from memory – he or she is likely to need several attempts to write a word correctly!

- When talking about letter sounds, try not to add too much of an *uh* or *er* sound. Say *mmm* instead of *muh* or *mer*, *ssss* instead of *suh* or *ser*. Saying letter sounds as carefully as possible will help your child when he or she is trying to build up or spell words – *her-a-der* doesn't sound much like 'had'!

- Talk about words: their meanings, how they sound, how they look and how they are spelled; but if your child gets restless or bored, stop. Enjoyment of the story, activity or book is essential if we want children to grow up valuing books and reading!